WAY TO GO KIDDO

WRITTEN AND ILLUSTRATED BY

ALAN HINES

Toddlers to Dodderers Publishing

In Honor of Love, Liberty and New Beginnings

Toddlers to Dodderers Publishing

www.toddlerstododdererspublishing.com

Quality Picture Books for Children and Seniors

WAY TO GO KIDDO

Marina Harris blew out the candles on her cake. She was vital, beautiful and had two grown children and three grandchildren. She lived in Albemarle, North Carolina and had many friends. Everyone loved the Harris family and they all wept on the day of Donald's funeral, three years earlier.

Marina adjusted relatively well, following her husband's death. He had made the necessary financial preparations so that she and the family would never have to worry. Despite an outpouring of support from family and friends, her heart held a void.

During World War II Marina Alfaro traveled to the United States from Bogota, Columbia to attend Shorter College in Rome, Georgia. She had been awarded a full scholarship to study voice there. Her father, a flourmill owner, reluctantly allowed her to leave home. Without hesitation, she accepted the opportunity. She made good grades, and was the best freshman soprano. Marina, who was more serious about school than dating, broke many men's hearts.

Meanwhile, Donald Harris was undergoing pre-flight training at the University of Georgia in Athens. He grew up in Atlanta and postponed his dream of opening a hardware store to enlist in the Navy.

I LEFT BOGATA FOR THE U.S.A. IN JULY of 1942.

CADET HARRIS DURING HIS PREFLIGHT TRAINING IN ATHENS, GA. FALL of 1942.

They met for the first time on a cool autumn evening. The Shorter College Choral Club, performed in the University of Georgia's auditorium. Marina sang the soprano lead in *Ave Maria*. Donald attended the concert and was captivated by her beauty and voice. Upon noticing the handsome cadet, she sang solely to him. Following the concert, he waited for her in the lobby.

Donald greeted her with enthusiastic applause and a hardy, boisterous, "Way to go kiddo." Marina smiled as he introduced himself. She reciprocated, and they fell into an awkward silence. Donald cleared his throat and asked her out for coffee. Without hesitation, Marina consented; and they were on their way to the diner, conversation, and romance.

Due to the uncertainty of war and the reality of unwanted separation, they expressed their love for one another. Initially, they exchanged letters and photographs. As war efforts intensified, he stopped writing to her.

Donald's training took him to the Midwest, and up and down the eastern seaboard. He earned his wings in Florida and while stationed in Massachusetts, flew a *Corsair F4U* off the coast, patrolling for enemy submarines.

On nocturnal missions, Donald witnessed the searing orange glow of the exhaust pipes and occasionally in storms, St. Elmo's fire arcing across the wings. These wonders, evoked feelings of awe and love for God, country and a beautiful woman; he could not get off of his mind.

The final assignment landed him on the *USS Midway* in Norfolk, Virginia. WWII ended late that summer and the world seemed safe again. Days later, Donald helped to commission the magnificent aircraft carrier.

DONALD BY CORSAIRS WITH "GULLWINGS" FOLDED UP.

TO MY DONALD

TE AMO! M

A PHOTO I SENT DONALD WHICH HE CARRIED IN HIS PLANE.

THE FLOWER DONALD PICKED FOR ME THE NIGHT WE FIRST MET.

DONALD IN THE COCKPIT OF HIS CORSAIR.

Before being discharged, he resumed his plans for opening a hardware store in Atlanta. Yet, he knew that visiting Marina was the top priority. He adored her and due to his negligence, feared he had lost her.

He put in a request for leave. When it was granted, he borrowed a car and drove to Rome to see her. Initially he had planned on calling, but opted for a surprise visit instead.

While searching for her, a variety of melodies emanated from the recital hall's practice rooms. This heightened his anticipation of their reunion. He looked through various windows and finally found Marina singing scales at the piano. Donald waited for silence and then rapped on the glass. The door squeaked open. Donald greeted her, "Way to go kiddo!"

Startled, Marina jumped and gasped. She scolded him for deserting her. Then with defiance, stated that he was too late and she was unavailable. Crestfallen, he left the building and was almost to the parking lot when he heard, "Donald wait!"

He turned around just in time to take Marina's full-body impact. The force of the collision laid him on his back. She showered him with kisses, exclaiming over and over, "I missed you and I love you!"

Donald dusted himself off, proposed, and she accepted. They planned to wed a few days after her graduation in the spring. Donald shared his entrepreneurial plans with her. Excited, Marina informed him of the numerous visits she and her friend Rose had made to Albemarle. She adored the people, as well as the quaint surroundings and suggested that they settle there. After being discharged, he made several trips to the small town and fell in love with the place.

While attending Marina's graduation, Donald met her family. A week later, the two married in a garden at Shorter College. Everyone said their goodbyes and the newlyweds headed for North Carolina.

Donald had already moved them into their cozy apartment on Montgomery Avenue. Following a two-day honeymoon, he stood in an empty building on Second Street that would become Harris Hardware.

Thanks to his GI Bill resources, a business loan and the sweat of his brow, Donald built a successful enterprise in a brief period of time. Marina helped by creating a well-stocked and thoughtful housewares department.

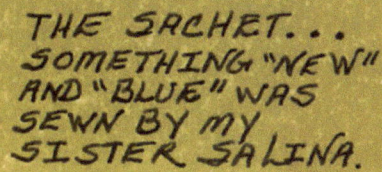

THE SACHET...
SOMETHING "NEW"
AND "BLUE" WAS
SEWN BY MY
SISTER SALINA.

THE CEREMONY WAS PERFORMED BY
PASTOR JOSHUA THORNE EARLY
SUMMER 1946. THE DRESS WAS "OLD"
AND "BORROWED" FROM MY MOM.

THE CAKE WAS
CREATED BY MY
FRIEND ROSE.

When Marina became pregnant, they purchased a suitable, vintage house on a hill. Marina gave birth to a baby girl, which they named Lorna. A few years later, they had a son named Jake.

Each day, she nurtured the children and made their home more comfortable and beautiful. Every night, Donald came home from the store tired, but spent time with his family until lights out. Despite her maternal demands, Marina also sang with the Central Methodist Church choir.

PICTURED (L-R)
ROBERT PICKLER
DONALD HARRIS
LORENZO SMITH
DAN YOUNGBLOOD

—HARRIS HARDWARE OPENS—

IN FRONT OF OUR HOME WITH 3 YEAR OLD LORNA
AND BABY BROTHER JAKE.

The family vacationed on South Carolina's coast every summer. When the children were young, they visited Norfolk, Virginia a few times to see the *USS Midway*, before she was relocated to Alameda, California.

While in college, the Harris kids helped their parents mind the store during summer breaks. After graduating, Lorna married, had two little girls, and moved to Charlotte, North Carolina. Jake, earned a business degree from UNC at Chapel Hill and returned home to assist with the family operation. Later he married, had a son and became the proud manager of Harris Hardware.

Donald retired from active participation in the business. One day on the golf course, a seemingly healthy Donald collapsed from a stroke. Despite what appeared to be a good recovery, a year later, he passed away peacefully while sleeping.

MOM AND DAD WITH THE GROWN UP CHILDREN AT MRYTLE BEACH.
(LEFT TO RIGHT) DONALD, JAKE, MARINA AND LORNA.

DONALD IN FULL
SWING AT
HILTON HEAD
ISLAND.

Marina spent a few years regrouping and getting her affairs in order. She missed Donald intensely, but chose to celebrate his life rather than mourn her loss.

One day after church, her pastor told her that the *USS Midway* was now a museum docked in San Diego, California. He learned of an annual Memorial Day event there and encouraged her to go. Marina decided to attend.

Once on board, the enormous crowd amazed her. Bands played as the veterans, their families and visitors held an immense celebration. Marina toured the ship and met some of Donald's comrades. When the festivities ended, she lingered alone at the bow.

Leaning on the chain railing, she looked out over the vast Pacific Ocean. She sensed Donald's presence and reflected on the abundant, blessed life they had shared. The sun was going down, so it was time to leave.

Marina was exiting the carrier and realized she had dropped her purse. Hastening back to find it, she saw the silhouette of a man approaching.

"Looking for this?" he inquired and offered her the pocket book. Winded, she grasped the strap and said, "Thank you."

Introductions followed. During the course of their conversation, they realized they had Donald in common and were both recently widowed. When Marina learned, he was Captain James Cook, she laughed. "I can't believe I'm with such a celebrity! You should be on the *Discovery*, not the *Midway*. I bet they treat you like a god in Hawaii."

"You almost have it right, Madame. I own and operate Captain Cook's Cuisine, over in Old Town. Our specialty is Hawaiian grub! As a-matter-of-fact, you have an open invitation to dine there at your leisure."

Without hesitation, Marina accepted his offer. Walking down the sunset bathed deck, she sensed that this was not only dinner with the Captain, but the beginning of a new voyage. As they passed the bridge, a soft breeze whirred around the observation tower. It caressed Mariana's left ear and whispered …

"WAY TO GO KIDDO"

Acknowledgments

My sincere appreciation to the following individuals whose knowledge and efforts contributed to the creation of this book.

Charles and Nancy Clark……………………………Editors

Frances Hines……………………………………Inspiration

Richard Coates………..……………*USS Midway* DOCENT

John Rivest……………………Shorter University Librarian

Jay Javan…………………………………Initial Layout Artist

Stephen Fitzgerald…………………………PDF File Creator

Suzanne LaValley-Hines…………………......My Everything

In loving memory of my Father, P.T. Hines, Jr.

An aviator and officer who helped
commission the *USS Midway* following WWII.

www.ingramcontent.com/pod-product-compliance
Lightning Source LLC
Chambersburg PA
CBHW041013170626
46815CB00003B/279

9 780984 049837